OGRE FUN

For my Mogre

— L.L.

Annick Press gratefully acknowledges the support of the Canada Council and the Ontario Arts Council.

Cataloguing in Publication Data

Lesynski, Loris
    Ogre fun

ISBN 1-55037-447-8 (bound)   ISBN 1-55037-446-X (pbk.)

I. Title.

PS8573.E79037 1997   jC813'.54   C97-930827-5
PZ7.L47.Og 1997

The art in this book was rendered in watercolour and coloured pencil.
The text was typeset in Utopia.

Distributed in Canada by:
  Firefly Books Ltd.
  3680 Victoria Park Avenue
  Willowdale, ON
  M2H 3K1

Published in the U.S.A. by
Annick Press (U.S.) Ltd.
Distributed in the U.S.A. by:
Firefly Books (U.S.) Inc.
P.O. Box 1338
Ellicott Station
Buffalo, NY 14205

Printed and bound in Canada by Kromar Printing Limited.

OGRE FUN

Written and illustrated
by Loris Lesynski

Annick Press
Toronto • New York

he ogre-boy named Gronny said,
"I'm absolutely bored.
How come we don't have ogre fun
the way we did before?"

The ogres sighed,
"Remember catching hiccups
from the troll?"

"Then itches from the witches
almost made us lose control!"

Hic! Hic!

Hic! Hic! Hic!
Hic!

"We've just about
run out of any creatures to attack.
It's **NO** fun for an ogre
catching something awful back."

But Gronny said, "I know, I'll go!"
for Gronny loved to roam.
"I'll find us someone safe to scare!"
—and off he flew from home.

Through the woods and dales he rambled,
hills and valleys he explored,
'til he found some little creatures—

—that he'd never seen before.

He watched them in the clearing as they scurried here and there.
All but one was lively.
They were perfect for a Scare.

He watched them catch a round thing
which they threw, and caught, and threw.

Little did he know that *he*
was catching something too.

Racing home to supper,
   Gron was bursting with delight.
He'd show the ogre grownups
   where to Scare
      tomorrow night.

Gronny was about to tell, when
   Mogre served the stew.

He gulped it down. And then
   the very *strangest* feeling grew...

It tickled most inside his throat.
   It prickled in his eyes—
a funny kind of tugging
   Gronny couldn't recognize.

It's what that little creature did—
   the one on second base.
Gronny had to do it too.
   It seemed inside his face!

He squished his face.
He squashed his face.
He tried to keep it shut.
He glued his mouth with jam inside
to keep it tighter
but—

—it opened like an oven door

for one ENORMOUS yawn

quite so big
it just about
obliterated Gron.

The ogres went hysterical!
  The babies started crying!
    The slugs-on-toast fell upside down,
      the sausages went flying.
        They'd never seen a yawn before.
          He heard his Mogre say—

—"Gronathon, you wretched boy,
you stop it RIGHT AWAY!"

But halfway through the words, her rosy lips
began to swell—
and stretched
into a yawn
as deep and dark
as any well.

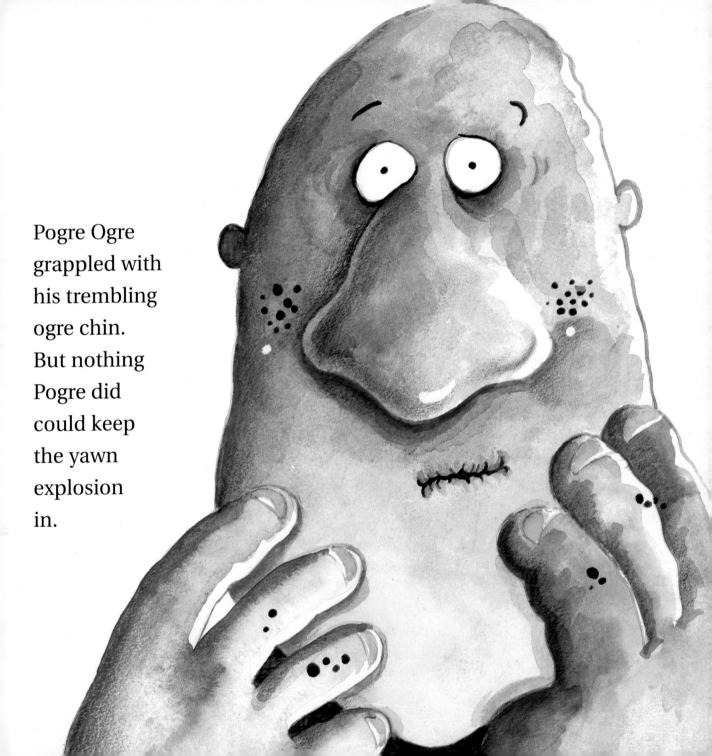

Pogre Ogre grappled with his trembling ogre chin. But nothing Pogre did could keep the yawn explosion in.

Gronny saw…

each ogre jaw…

begin to fall—and *drop.*

They'd never yawned—not once before—

and now they couldn't stop.

They couldn't finish supper—
they couldn't use their spoons.

Their ogre cheeks puffed in and out
like lumpy green balloons.

They spilled their ogre cocoa when
they bumped into the wall.

When bugs flew in their open yaps,
they couldn't sleep at all.

"*Yaaww*–ful, *yaaaaawwww*–ful!"
    Mogre yawned. "Disaster for the pack!
    I think these must have come with you,
    so Gronny—give them BACK."

Worried sick and yawning,
    Gronny sped to seek advice
from those dreadful little creatures
    who had looked so very nice.

But the playground
    in the moonlight was
        as empty as a plate.

He spied the nearest cottage…

    …and he tiptoed
        to the gate…

Dare he press up closer to
    the window with a light?

Oh no—the creatures, yawning,
    were preparing for the night.

One by one the children saw
his yawning ogre face,
and screamed, *and screamed,*
and screamed, **and SCREAMED,**
AND SCREAMED
apart the place.

Gronny thought
the screaming was
just bigger yawns,
with noise.

"I'll catch that too!"
he cried in dread, but
faced the girls and boys.

If he couldn't stop
his yawning,
would he ever roam again?
The nasty little creatures made
another scream—
and then—

Gronny made it
back to them
**as loudly
as he could.**

And suddenly—
his yawning
stopped.

He bolted for the wood.

At home again, he stayed outside.
The ogres heard his plea:
"Don't let me see you yawn again,
but do the same as me."
Then Gronny screamed.
They screamed in turn,
for how long, no one knew—

—but when the screaming ended,
the yawning ended too.

"How beautiful a sound, my son!"
said Mogre from the heart.
"You saved the day. And brought a song.
But still, we must depart.
We only want to scare someone,
not itch…
or hic…
or yawn.
None of that was fun at all.
It's time that we were gone."

Away the ogres wandered, sure to find
a better home.

They loved their "song" and Gronny got
a perfect chance to roam.

And this is why you seldom see
an ogre here today.
And how a tiny, moany yawn
or an **open, growly, groany yawn**
is a scary-to-an-ogre yawn
and keeps them far away.

So remember, if you meet one
and his gruesome gob is wide—
you can save yourself by running

or

by yawning…

you decide.

• THE END •